With thanks to Holly Webb and the
9th Tilehurst Brownies and Guides

STRIPES PUBLISHING
An imprint of Magi Publications
1 The Coda Centre, 189 Munster Road,
London SW6 6AW

A paperback original. First published in Great Britain in 2011
Published by arrangement with Girlguiding UK
Brownie logo, uniforms and badges copyright © Girlguiding UK
Text copyright © Caroline Plaisted, 2011. Illustrations copyright © Katie Wood, 2011

ISBN: 978-1-84715-162-9

A CIP catalogue record for this book is available
from the British Library.

Printed and bound in the UK.
2 4 6 8 10 9 7 5 3 1

Find out more about the author at
www.carolineplaisted.com

Brownies

Book Bonanza

Stripes

Meet the Brownies

Katie

Katie, Grace's twin, is super sporty and likes to play games and win. She wants to get every Brownie badge and her Six is Foxes!

Jamila

Jamila's got too many brothers, so she loves Brownies because NO BOYS ARE ALLOWED! Jamila is a Badger!

Ellie

Awesome at art and crafts, Ellie used to be a Rainbow and likes making new friends. Ellie is a Hedgehog!

Charlie

Animal-crazy Charlie has a guinea pig called Nibbles. She loves Brownie quizzes and Pow Wows. Her Six is Squirrels!

Grace

Grace is Katie's twin sister and she's ballet bonkers. Grace enjoys going on Brownie outings, and she is a Rabbit!

Chapter 1

The 1st Badenbridge Brownies had just
settled down in their Brownie Ring after a
quick game of Traffic Lights. It was Pow
Wow time and the girls were eager to hear
each other's news.

Vicky, one of the Brownie Leaders,
smiled at the Sixer of the Badgers who had
her hand up. "Yes, Izzy," she said.

"It's World Book Day in four weeks' time
and we're going to celebrate it at school!"
Izzy announced.

Lots of the Brownies went to Badenbridge
Primary with Izzy, and they nodded in
agreement.

"We're dressing up as our favourite book characters at the school I go to," said Bethany.

"So are we!" exclaimed all the other Brownies.

"Even the teachers are dressing up!" Lucy added.

"That sounds fun," said Vicky.

"We're doing a writing competition at school as well," Katie said excitedly. She loved competitions.

"We've been given a title – *The Magic Shoes* – and we all have to make up a story around it," explained Jamila.

"I've already started mine," said Faith.

"You're quick – we were only told about it yesterday!" Boo exclaimed, and the Brownies laughed.

"Perhaps we could do something for World Book Day at Brownies too," wondered Vicky.

"Hmmm," said Sam. "I wonder what though? Anyone got any ideas?"

"I know!" said Emma, who was the Sixer of the Foxes and one of the oldest Brownies. "We could do the Booklover badge!"

There was a murmur of interest from around the Ring.

"Have any of you already done the Booklover badge?" asked Vicky. "I can't remember anyone doing it for a while."

All the girls shook their heads.

"Well, then the whole unit could work on it together, if you wanted to," Sam suggested.

"I did the Booklover badge when I was a Brownie," said Daisy, who was a Guide who came to help out at Brownies. "I really enjoyed it."

"What did you have to do?" asked Danuta.

"I remember having to read some books and then talk about them with a tester," Daisy replied. "That was my favourite bit about the badge. And I made a bookmark and learned how to make a cover for a book. I also showed I knew how to use a reference book, and made a poster about the library. There was lots to do, but it was all good fun."

"So, do you think you'd like to do the Booklover badge then?" asked Vicky.

"Yes, please!" all the Brownies replied.

"Great," said Sam. "We'd better get started on it soon then. Perhaps you could have a think about which books you'd like to be tested on? You can use a few books you've already read, and choose a couple of new ones too. Vicky and I will test you on some books, but you could ask someone like your teacher to test you on the others, if you like."

"Don't forget the Brownie Book Club on the Brownies website too," Daisy added. "It has reviews from other Brownies on it and lots of suggestions for books and authors to discover."

"Good idea," said Vicky. "Does anyone else have any book ideas to share?"

Abebi, one of the newest Brownies, put up her hand. "At my old school, an author came to talk to us about his books," she said. "Could we ask an author to come to Brownies, do you think?"

"That would be so cool," agreed Grace.

The hall filled with excited chatter as the Brownies discussed which of their favourite authors they would like to meet.

"I love the books Holly Webb writes about animals," said Charlie, who wanted to be a vet. "They're brilliant!"

Jamila nodded. "The ones about the naughty puppy are my favourites."

"Mine too!" said Pip.

"Do you know her books?" Charlie asked the Leaders.

"Yes, we do," said Sam. "Actually, we've met Holly."

"You've met Holly Webb?" yelped Charlie. "How? Where?"

"At a Leaders' Conference about a year ago," said Vicky, smiling. "Holly is a Guide Leader with a unit close to here."

"Wow!" said Charlie, impressed. "Hey, could we ask her to visit us?"

"Oh, please say yes!" the Brownies urged.

"Well, it would depend on how busy she is…" Sam pointed out.

"…But we could write to her and see what she says," said Vicky.

"Yes!" the Brownies cheered.

"Well then," said Vicky, turning to a fresh

piece of paper on her clipboard and taking the lid off her pen. "What shall we say?"

"We should tell her we love her books!" suggested Charlie.

Everyone laughed, and soon all the girls were chipping in with ideas of what to write. When they'd finished, Vicky read the letter back to them.

Dear Holly,

We are the 1st Badenbridge Brownies. We'll be celebrating World Book Day by working for our Booklover badge. We love reading and we have read lots of your books. They're great!

We would really like to meet an author and ask her how she gets the ideas for her stories. The author we would most like to meet is you! Vicky and Sam, our Leaders, told us that they had met you at a conference. They said you live near Badenbridge and we wondered if you would be able to come and see us. We would like to include you in our celebration of World Book Day.

Please, please, please come and see us!

Lots of love from all of the 1st Badenbridge Brownies.

The girls all exchanged excited smiles and crossed their fingers for luck. It would be brilliant if she came!

"I'll make sure that the letter goes in the post to Holly tomorrow," said Vicky. "But now, how about we carry on with our literary theme and have a go at book title Charades."

"Yes, please!" replied the Brownies. They loved Charades. It was a game where each of the Sixes had to take it in turns to mime the name of something – it could be a book, a film, or a television programme – and the rest of the unit had to guess what it was.

"Get into your Sixes and Vicky and I will come round and whisper which book title we'd like you to mime," said Sam. "You can have five minutes to think about it, and the Foxes can go first."

15

A short while later, the Brownies settled down on the floor with the Foxes standing in front of them. The Foxes' challenge was to mime *The BFG*, and it took ages for the others to work out that Emma wasn't a giraffe but a giant! But at last Megan guessed it and so her Six, the Squirrels, went next.

Sam had asked them to act out *The Worst Witch*, so they all whizzed around the hall on pretend broomsticks. The other Brownies immediately worked out that they were witches, but it was Caitlin who figured out that the reason Ashvini kept dropping her "broomstick" was because she was the worst witch!

The Rabbits went next and did an elaborate ghostly mime for *Spook School*, which Amy in the Hedgehogs guessed because she had just read the first book in the series.

The Hedgehogs had been asked to mime *Where the Wild Things Are*, and Lauren pretended to be Mum telling off Charlie, who was Max. Charlie stomped off to her pretend bedroom, and then sailed off to join the Wild Things. The Hedgehogs loved roaring silently at the Brownies, and were sad when Jamila guessed what their book was and they had to stop!

The Badgers began by jumping thirteen times to represent the number of times the clock chimed in *Tom's Midnight Garden*. Next, Izzy pretended to be Tom exploring the garden, and Daisy guessed the title straight away but wouldn't tell the rest of the unit what it was. It was Katie who got it

in the end – she was thrilled.

"Well done, Katie. That was a really hard one to guess," Vicky said. "My cheeks ache from laughing – what a talented bunch you are!"

"Yes," agreed Sam, looking at her watch. "Now, it's almost time to go home, I'm afraid!"

"Nooooo!" the girls sighed sadly.

Vicky smiled. "We'll post our letter off to Holly and keep our fingers crossed that she will be able to come and see us before World Book Day."

"In the meantime," added Sam, "don't forget to take a look in your badge books to find out more about the Booklover badge."

"And now," said Vicky, "let's join hands and sing 'Brownies Bells' to end our meeting."

Chapter 2

The best friends were still excited about everything they were doing for World Book Day when they went round to Jamila's house for tea after school the next day. Jamila's mum had laid out cheese sandwiches and chocolate cupcakes.

"I wish I could write a story about food for school," Grace giggled, as she leaned over to pick up a second sandwich.

"So what are you going to write about?" asked Ellie.

"My story's about some magic running shoes," announced Katie.

"What a surprise!" giggled Jamila. "I'm writing about some shoes that take me to see my great grandma in Pakistan."

"That's a brilliant idea," said Ellie. "Mine's about a pair of boots that take me to visit Leonardo Da Vinci — you know, the famous painter from centuries ago? I'm doing some pictures for it as well."

"You mean it's a time travel-story?" Grace grinned. "Cool! Mine's about magic ballet shoes, but I haven't worked out exactly what's going to happen in it yet."

"And I don't even have a clue where to begin!" wailed Charlie. "I'm hopeless at writing!"

"No, you're not," said Jamila, giving her friend a hug. "You wrote that brilliant poem for the Brownie Show, remember?"

Charlie had written about her guinea pig Nibbles for the Brownie Show the previous year. She had also brought him along for the audience to see – but he must have got stage fright, because he managed to escape from his cage just before Charlie's performance! Luckily, he was soon found again.

"It took me ages, though," said Charlie. "I wish Holly Webb was coming to see us next week – she'd be able to give me some ideas…"

"Mr Cole said to write about something you're interested in," said Grace. Mr Cole was their teacher.

"How about writing a story about Nibbles?" suggested Jamila.

"I suppose I could…" Charlie said thoughtfully. "Except he doesn't wear any shoes!"

They all giggled.

"I know!" said Ellie. "Remember how Nibbles went missing when you brought him to the show? Well, how about he escapes again in this story? Maybe he could hide in a pair of magic shoes?"

"Yes!" Charlie grinned. "That could be the start of my story."

"You see," said Jamila. "Talking always helps work things out."

"Speaking of working things out," said Katie, "I can't decide which book character to come as on World Book Day."

"I'm thinking about being Alice from *Alice in Wonderland*," said Jamila. "I love the dress she wears in the illustrations, and my mum's got a pinny like Alice's that she's going to lend me."

"You'd look great as Alice," said Grace, who hadn't read the book, but had seen the film. "I wondered about dressing up as a character from this book called *Ballet Shoes*. There's a girl called Posy Fossil in it who is an orphan, and the only thing she has of her mother's is a pair of ballet shoes. It's such a sad story – but she ends up being the best dancer ever, so it has a happy ending!"

The others agreed that Grace would be perfect as Posy.

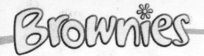

"What about you, Charlie?" asked Grace. "Any ideas?"

"Doctor Doolittle, of course!" she exclaimed.

The others giggled – it was typical of Charlie to choose a character that loved animals.

"So, who should I be?" wondered Katie.

"How about Hermione Granger," Ellie replied. "I've got an old cloak in my dressing-up box that I could lend you. And you could make a wand to cast spells with!"

Katie liked that idea. She waved an imaginary wand bossily in the air and looked just like Hermione. *"Expelliarmus!"* she said, making her friends laugh.

"Perfect!" said Ellie. "And I'm going to be Pippi Longstocking. You remember we read it in school last year?"

The friends couldn't forget it! It was about a girl with red hair who had superhuman strength and loads of adventures – it was a great book.

"Brilliant!" Grace said. "You've got just the right hair for the part."

Ellie grinned. "Mum's going to find me some stripey socks to wear and work out how to do my hair so it sticks out like Pippi's!"

"Hey – what book character do you think Mr Cole will dress up as?" Katie wondered.

"Dumbledore!" the others all said at once, and then burst out laughing.

Jamila sighed. "I can't wait to see everyone's outfits… Oh! We should get together to work on our costumes the weekend before World Book Day."

"Yes!" agreed the others.

"You could come round to my house –

I'm sure my mum would help us make any props we need. I'll ask her if that would be OK," said Ellie.

"Hey, has anyone looked up the Booklover badge yet?" Grace asked.

"Not yet," said Jamila. "Why don't we go and take a look in my badge book now?"

The girls cleared away their plates and glasses and hurried upstairs to Jamila's room.

"It says we've got to talk to our tester about four books we've enjoyed," said Katie, quickly scanning the page.

"Do you think Mr Cole might test us on some?" wondered Jamila.

"I should think so," Grace replied. "And it says here that we need to choose two more books by different authors with our tester."

The girls read through all the information in the badge book and discovered that they would also have to show how to look after a book and explain to their tester how to use a reference book.

"There's stuff about using the library too," pointed out Ellie.

"Katie and I were talking last night about going to the bookshop on Saturday morning," said Grace. "We got some book tokens at Christmas and thought now might

be a good time to use them."

"Perhaps Mum and Dad could take all of us?" suggested Katie.

The others thought it was a great idea, and decided to ask their parents about it as soon as they got home.

"Right, let's finish off those last few cupcakes in the kitchen," said Jamila. "Race you downstairs!"

Chapter 3

The girls met up in the playground before school started the next day.

"My mum said I could come book shopping on Saturday," Jamila said excitedly.

"Mine too!" said Charlie and Ellie at the same time, and everyone laughed. The girls agreed to meet up outside the bookshop at eleven o'clock.

Then, at breaktime, the five friends asked Mr Cole if he would be prepared to test them on some of their books for their badge. He said he'd be happy to, and they arranged the test for a lunch break in three weeks' time. Mr Cole also asked how they were getting on

with their Magic Shoes stories. It was only
Charlie who hadn't started writing yet, but she
promised she would start on it soon.

The next morning, everyone in the
playground was full of excitement; it was
Friday! The best friends were especially excited
about going book shopping the next day. Katie
and Grace were going to use their book tokens
and the others had raided their piggy banks for
enough money to buy a book each.

"And Mum said that she'd take us for lunch
in the bookshop café afterwards," said Katie.

"What could be better?" said Jamila.
"Food and books!"

"There are so many to choose from!" Katie
exclaimed, as she stood in
front of a brightly coloured

book display the next morning. The best friends had been dropped off in the children's department by Katie and Grace's mum, who had then gone to browse in a different part of the shop.

"I want them all!" said Charlie.

"Me too!" the others agreed.

Just then, a bookseller came over to speak to them. "Hello there. I'm Anna. Are you looking for anything in particular?"

"We're doing our Booklover badge at Brownies," Ellie explained, "and we'd each like to choose a new book for our badge work."

"Oh, I did my Booklover badge when I was a Brownie!" Anna said.

"Cool!" said Charlie.

As they browsed the shelves, Anna chatted with the girls about what kind of books they liked and suggested other stories that she thought they might enjoy. The best friends all found loads of books they wanted to read, and it was really difficult to choose just one. Eventually, once all five friends had made their decisions, they went over to the till. As they paid for their books, they told Anna all about what they were doing to celebrate World Book Day, both at school and at Brownies.

"Excellent," said Anna. "Tell you what —
why don't I nip into the office and see if I've
got some things you could take back to
Brownies, to help you celebrate reading?"

The girls exchanged puzzled glances —
what did she mean?

When Anna returned, she was carrying a
huge pile of bookmarks and a couple of book
posters, which she gave to them. "Will these
be useful?"

"Yes, thanks!" the best friends chorused.

"You're welcome! Good luck with your
badge work — and enjoy your books," Anna
replied.

Just then, Katie and Grace's mum came
over.

"Hungry?" she asked.

"Yes!" the five friends replied at once.

"Come on then — let's get some lunch."

As the girls munched on their sandwiches, Katie and Grace's mum asked them about the books they'd chosen.

"I picked a book about animals being rescued in the wild," Charlie said.

"No surprise there then!" Ellie laughed. "Mine's about fairies. What about you, Grace?"

"I bought a book of short stories set in winter," she explained. "Each one is by a different author."

"Cool," said Jamila. "My book's about a girl who's in a band."

Katie grinned. "I chose a book all about the Olympic games and its history."

"Sounds like you've all got books that are perfect for you," Katie and Grace's mum said.

"Now, I'm just wondering if any of you could manage a piece of chocolate cake before you start reading…?"

"Yes, please!" they all replied.

Chapter 4

When the girls met up at school on Monday morning, they chatted excitedly about what they'd read over the weekend.

"I can't wait to find out what happens next in my book – I'll read some more when I get home tonight," said Ellie.

"Me too," agreed Grace. "I haven't finished mine yet because I was busy writing my Magic Shoes story."

"Oh, I finished my book," said Charlie. "It was so good, I couldn't put it down! I'll have to do some of my writing tonight."

"Can I read your book if you've finished it?" asked Katie.

"Sure," said Charlie. "I'll bring it to school for you tomorrow."

The others thought that sounded like a great idea, and agreed to bring their books to school when they'd finished them so they could swap.

At their meeting on Tuesday night, all the Brownies sat in the Ring and told Vicky and Sam what badge work they'd already done for their Booklover badge. Most of them had selected some books to read, and they talked about what they had chosen with those who were still deciding. Then Katie told everyone about their trip to the bookshop.

"Anna the bookseller gave us some bookmarks for everyone," Grace added, handing them around the Ring.

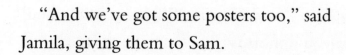

"And we've got some posters too," said Jamila, giving them to Sam.

"They're terrific," said Vicky, looking at one of the brightly coloured bookmarks, which featured a new series of books about a mermaid. "And a bit of a coincidence as well."

"Making a bookmark is part of our badge work," Sam explained. "And we thought we'd make some after our Pow Wow."

"Yaaaaay!" said all the Brownies, who loved making things.

"What else are we going to do tonight?" asked Jasmine.

"Oooh!" Charlie shot up her arm before

either Vicky or Sam could answer. "Please! Did you post our letter to Holly Webb?"

Vicky smiled. "I did."

There was a murmur of excitement around the Ring.

"I wonder when we'll hear back from her?" said Sukia.

"Actually..." said Sam. "We already have!"

"What did she say?" Charlie asked.

"Is she coming?" asked Katie.

Vicky and Sam smiled and then nodded.

"Yessss!" the Brownies cheered and began to chat excitedly.

Vicky and Sam both put up their right hands. Gradually, the Brownies noticed and did the same, falling silent.

"Thank you, girls," said Vicky. "So, Holly has kindly agreed to come and see us in a couple of weeks' time."

"And we need you all to think of what you would like to ask her when she visits," said Sam.

"In a minute you can go to your Six tables," Vicky continued. "Daisy has laid out some blank bookmarks ready for you to design and colour in. While you are doing that, chat with your Six about the questions you'd like to put to Holly. Try to come up with the most interesting questions you possibly can."

"Ready?" asked Sam.

The Brownies nodded.

"Then off you go!"

All around the hall, the Brownies talked noisily as they decorated their bookmarks. They drew and coloured in pictures of

Brownies reading books, their favourite book covers and characters, and other things that reminded them of reading. And while they worked, they chattered excitedly about what to ask Holly.

Twenty minutes later, they gathered back in the Ring to show their finished bookmarks and discuss the questions they'd come up with.

"So, who would like to go first?" asked Sam.

Loads of hands went up.

"Just the Sixers, please!" Sam laughed.
"Lauren – you go first."

Lauren, the Sixer of the Hedgehogs,

 announced that her Six wanted
to ask Holly where she did her
writing. "And we also want to
know how long it takes her to
write a book," she added.

Next, it was Molly's turn to speak for the
Rabbits. Her Six wanted
to ask Holly how many
books she'd written.

Izzy, the Sixer of the

 Badgers, said that they would
like to know if Holly had
always known she wanted
to be a writer, even when
she was at school.

The Squirrels were the next Six to talk

about what they planned to ask. Megan said that they would like to know how she got her ideas for stories and if she owned any of the animals that featured in her books.

Finally, Emma said that the Foxes had decided to ask Holly if she wrote her books by hand or used a computer, and also if she had a special time of day when she wrote.

"Those are great questions," said Vicky. "You've clearly put a lot of thought into them."

"Now," said Sam, looking at her watch. "It's nearly time to go…"

"Awww!" wailed the Brownies.

"Next week, we'll be making posters about the library for our badge work," said Sam.

"Could you find out some information to put on them? There are guidelines in your badge books."

"And could you all bring a reference book with you next week," said Vicky. "We'll be investigating indexes and contents pages. Then we can do our first bit of testing."

The Brownies grinned, knowing that if they kept up their badge work, they'd soon be awarded their badges.

"But now it's time to go home," said Sam. "Come on – let's sing 'Brownie Bells'."

And the tired but happy Brownies stood up, linked hands and began to sing.

Chapter 5

On Thursday, the best friends went round to Charlie and Boo's house for tea after school. While they waited for the sisters' mum to prepare some food, Boo showed Charlie and the others a website she'd found. It was all about World Book Day.

"There's loads of stuff to do on here," Boo said, as they surfed the site.

They found games to play, and information about authors and their websites, as well as activity sheets. "Hey," said Grace, "what's that about Book Aid International – over there?"

"Hmmm, I don't know," said Boo, clicking on the link.

The girls crowded around the screen and watched as the computer loaded another page.

"It's a charity," said Boo.

"Oh yes," said Jamila, pointing to a section on the screen. "Look – they help children in schools in poor countries."

The girls discovered that Book Aid International sent books to libraries in schools, refugee camps, hospitals, universities and communities in twelve countries in Africa.

"It says here that a donation of two pounds

pays for a book to be sent to a library that can't afford to buy its own," said Ellie.

"Wow," sighed Katie, thinking about their own school library, which was full of books. "Imagine being at a school with no books…"

"That would be awful," agreed Charlie.

"Do you think we could do something to help?" said Ellie.

The girls thought for a moment about all the fun they were having at school and in Brownies with books.

"Perhaps we could send them our old books?" wondered Jamila.

"No…" Boo said, scanning down the screen. "They don't want old books. Just donations to buy new ones."

"I know!" exclaimed Grace. "We could hold a book sale at Brownies for Book Aid International!"

"But where would we get the books from?" wondered Ellie.

"We could swap them!" said Katie. "Like we're going to do with the books we bought last weekend. Everyone who comes to the sale would bring a book with them and swap it for another one. That way, we'll have lots of books!"

"But wait," said Charlie. "If we're just swapping books, how do we raise money for Book Aid International?"

"Ooh, I know! Pay an entry fee!" Ellie suggested. "Everyone could pay one pound to get in."

"Good idea," the others agreed.

"And if we invite all our friends, hopefully we can raise lots of money," said Grace.

"We'd better talk about it with Vicky and Sam on Tuesday," said Boo.

Just then, Charlie and Boo's mum called them down for tea. Boo closed the internet browser and the girls trooped downstairs to eat, chatting excitedly about their new idea.

They were still thinking about the book swap idea and Book Aid International at lunchtime the next day. "We're really lucky, aren't we?" said Ellie. "We don't have to worry about finding a book to read because we can go to the bookshop or the library. And in school, we've got lots of books to choose from."

The others nodded.

"Talking of libraries," said Katie, "we've got to find out more about the library for Brownies next week."

"Oh yes, for our posters," agreed Jamila. "Do you think we could go tomorrow?"

"And maybe we could ask the librarian if she could help by testing us on two of our books for our badge too," said Charlie.

"Great idea," said Grace. "Let's ask our parents about it as soon as we get home!"

The friends met up in the children's section of the library on Saturday morning. Catherine the librarian had just finished putting some books back on the shelves when she spotted the girls looking at the reference books.

"What are you looking for today, then?" Catherine asked.

They explained all about their Booklover badge and the work they needed to do on reference books at their next Brownie meeting.

"Do you have any hobbies?" said Catherine. "We could see if we've got some reference books that tie into your interests."

"I like music – and cooking!" said Jamila. "Where would I find books about those sorts of things?"

Catherine showed the girls how the numbers stuck on the spines of the books represented the subject the books were about.

After pointing Jamila in the right direction, she spoke to the others about their favourite things. Soon Katie was looking in the sports section, Grace had found the ballet books, Charlie was leafing through a book on pet care, and Ellie was browsing the craft books. Once the five friends had chosen their books, they took them over to the desk to check them out, and chatted to Catherine about their badge.

"Do you think you might be able to test us on two of our books?" asked Katie.

"I'd be very happy to do that." Catherine smiled. "Just pop into the library when you're ready. Is there anything else I can help with?"

The girls explained that they'd be making

posters about the library at their next Brownie meeting.

"Well, why don't you each take one of these leaflets?" suggested Catherine, handing them out. They had all the details of the library opening times and what things could be borrowed. "You know we've got a great selection of DVDs as well. The latest *Nanny McPhee* film is just in…"

"*Nanny McPhee*?" exclaimed Grace. "Can I borrow that on my library card?"

Catherine nodded. "And it's even a movie based on a book," she said. "Maybe that would link in with your badge work too?"

"You could all come round tomorrow and watch it," Ellie said to the others.

"Yes, please!" the best friends replied.

The following afternoon, as promised, the girls went round to watch *Nanny McPhee* at Ellie's house. "That was great," said Jamila, as they sipped milk and nibbled on chocolate chip biscuits after the film ended.

"I might see if I can find a copy of the book it was based on," said Grace. "I love magical stories."

"Speaking of magical stories," said Ellie, "how long do we have to finish our Magic Shoes stories?"

"Mr Cole said we had to hand them in on the Wednesday before World Book Day, so in about ten days' time," Grace replied.

"Oh no!" exclaimed Charlie. "I've hardly started mine."

"Wow, Charlie," said Katie. "I've already finished mine. And so has Grace."

Charlie blushed. "It's not my fault I haven't

had time to finish it," she said. "I've been re-reading Holly Webb's books in time for her visit. And I wanted to make sure I was ready for being tested on my books for the badge…"

"Don't worry," said Grace, putting her arm around Charlie. "If you do some every night next week, it'll soon be finished."

"Maybe we could help you with it some more after school?" said Jamila.

"Thanks," said Charlie, smiling. She felt really lucky to have such good friends.

Chapter 6

On Monday afternoon, Ellie went home with Charlie and Boo after school to help Charlie with her story. Ellie suggested that someone could put the shoes on, but Charlie pointed out that Nibbles might get squashed if that happened! Then they came up with the idea of having the shoes accidentally packed in a sports bag and being put in the boot of a car.

Charlie liked that, and she wrote another half-page of her story before Ellie's mum arrived. Before Ellie left, she, Charlie and Boo showed their mums the books they'd borrowed, and explained to them how the indexes and contents pages worked.

"Looks like you're well on your way to getting that badge," said Ellie's mum.

"We've still got to be tested by Mr Cole on two of the books we've read," Charlie said.

"And Catherine at the library," added Ellie.

"Don't forget Vicky and Sam are testing us on two as well," said Boo.

"Golly," said Charlie and Boo's mum. "I'm exhausted just thinking about it!"

"So, who's got news?" asked Vicky, looking around the Brownie Ring on Tuesday night.

"Please, Vicky!" said Ellie. "Jamila, Charlie, Boo, Katie, Grace and I had an idea for World Book Day."

The six girls explained about finding the Book Aid International website and raising money by having a book swap. Boo handed

Vicky some information about Book Aid

International that she'd
printed off the website.
"Hmm," said Vicky,
reading the details.
"It sounds like an excellent
cause…"
"But there's not
much time until World
Book Day," said Sam.
"I'm not sure we'd be able to get everything
organized in time."

"And where would we hold it?" Vicky said.

"Here!" declared Katie.

"Please!" begged Ellie. "If we all promise
to help, we could do it!"

All the other Brownies were just as
enthusiastic, and they chipped in with ideas.

"My family would come," said Caitlin.

"I could ask my mum and dad if we could donate some of my old books," added Tayla-Ann. "I'm sure they'd say yes."

"We could make posters to tell everyone about it," Amy suggested.

"And call it a Book Bonanza!" said Megan.

"You Brownies always have such good ideas!" Vicky laughed.

The Brownies looked at Sam anxiously. Was she going to say no?

"Well," said Sam, "we could try…"

"Yessss!" the girls cheered.

"But only if school says we can use this hall," Vicky continued. "And only if you absolutely promise to help us."

"We will," the Brownies promised.

"OK then," said Sam. "We'll look into arranging the venue for the Book Bonanza. But tonight we've got Booklover badge

work to do. Have you all brought your reference books with you?"

The Brownies nodded.

"Good," said Vicky. "We'll test you in your Sixes, but that will take some time. So, while you're waiting for us, you can get busy on your posters about the library."

"Did you all manage to find some information to put on them?" asked Sam.

"Yes!" the girls replied.

"Great," said Vicky. "Make your posters as colourful and interesting as you can. Imagine you are trying to encourage other children to come to the library for the first time – and don't forget to tell them when it's open and what they can find there."

"Right – let's get to work!" said Sam.

Within moments, the hall was buzzing with busy Brownies. The girls showed their

Leaders that they knew how to use the contents and index pages of their reference books and retrieve information from them. And when they weren't being tested, they chatted happily about the Book Bonanza as they worked on their posters at their Six tables.

Once they had finished decorating their posters, the Brownies played an energetic skipping game, and then gathered back in the Ring to close their meeting.

"Well, I don't know about you, Brownies, but I'm exhausted," Vicky said.

"Time to head home, I think," Sam added. "Now, don't forget that next week we've got an important visitor coming to see us!"

"Holly Webb!" exclaimed Charlie. She could hardly wait!

Chapter 7

"I can't believe we're going to meet Holly next week!" said Charlie, as the friends gathered in the playground the next morning. "Do you think she'll sign one of my books?"

"I'm sure she will," Grace replied.

"A whole week seems ages to wait…" Charlie sighed.

"I know," said Jamila, "but there are so many things to do for World Book Day and our Booklover badge that I'm sure the time will go really quickly."

"And you're coming round to my house on Saturday to work on our book costumes," Ellie pointed out. "That'll be fun!"

"You wait till you see my Doctor Doolittle trousers," said Charlie. "They're really wacky."

"And we're being tested on two of our books by Mr Cole at lunchtime today, aren't we?" Jamila pointed out.

Katie nodded. "I had a quick look over my books again this morning to make sure I know everything there is to know about them."

"You'll be fine," said Grace. "Mr Cole won't ask anything really difficult."

"Once we've done our tests with Mr Cole and Catherine at the library, what badge work will we have left to do?" Ellie asked.

"Well, we did the reference book work last night. And we've made our bookmarks," said Katie.

"And the library poster," added Charlie.

"So we've still got the book care section," said Jamila.

"And Vicky and Sam still have to test us on two books – that will be six all together," said Grace.

"Phew!" said Charlie. "I've done all my reading, but I still haven't finished my Magic Shoes story. I'll probably do it when I get home tonight. I just hope I pass my book test with Mr Cole first!"

Grace and Jamila played on their own after they'd eaten their lunch, while Charlie, Katie and Ellie sat in the classroom with Mr Cole, being tested.

"You were in there for ages!" Jamila said when they finally emerged.

"How was it?" asked Grace.

"It was fun! Mr Cole is so nice, it didn't seem like a test at all," said Katie.

"He asked us what we'd liked about our books," said Charlie.

"And to describe the stories and the characters in them," Ellie added.

"He wanted to know which character we'd like to be," said Katie. "And then he gave us these!"

Katie handed Jamila her certificate, and Jamila read it aloud.

This certificate is awarded to

Katie

who has been successfully
tested on two books for her
Booklover badge by Mr Cole.

"Well done!" said Grace.

"Come on, Grace – it's our turn now,"
Jamila said.

"See you later – and good luck!" Katie,
Ellie and Charlie called, as Grace and Jamila
headed for the classroom.

Jamila and Grace passed their tests with
flying colours and, not satisfied with having
completed one more part of their badge
work, the five best friends started on their
next two books straight away.

Wednesday and Thursday evening were
spent reading happily. And then, at the end
of school on Friday, Mr Cole reminded the
class that their Magic Shoes stories had to
be handed in by the following Wednesday
morning.

"Have you finished your story yet, Charlie?" Grace asked, as the five friends walked out to meet their parents in the playground.

"Almost," said Charlie. But what she didn't add was that she was struggling to come up with an ending.

"Great!" said Grace. "Oh, there's Mum. See you all at Ellie's house tomorrow!"

"Bye!" Jamila, Charlie and Ellie waved, as the twins hurried off.

On Saturday morning, the five friends gathered in Ellie's living room, and excitedly set about assembling their costumes for World Book Day. Ellie's mum was there to help too.

As Doctor Doolittle, Charlie needed to wear narrow checked trousers. Her mum had found a pair of yellow leggings that she and Charlie had felt-tipped the checks on to earlier that week. She tried them on, then put on a white school shirt and a red V-necked jumper, with her sister's black jacket over the top.

"This is what he looks like in the book," said Charlie, showing the others the cover.

"All you need is the blue neck tie, a top hat and a watch on a chain," pointed out Ellie. "I could help you make the watch and top hat out of cardboard, if you like."

"Brilliant!" said Charlie. "Thanks. So what about your costume? Did you find some stripey tights?"

69

"Ta-da!" Ellie replied, holding up some amazing multicoloured tights. "Then I'm going to wear this pinafore dress – we're going to sew a few patches on to it," said Ellie, showing them a pale blue dress. "And Mum's going to do my hair in sticky-out plaits on the day!"

Meanwhile, Katie had slipped into her school skirt and shirt, and asked Ellie's mum to help her do up her tie. She pulled her "wand" (a stick she'd found in the garden) out of her bag and slipped Ellie's dressing-up cloak round her shoulders.

"*Wingardium leviosa!*" she commanded, pointing her wand at the table.

"You look great!" said Charlie.

"Yes," agreed Grace. "But you'd look even better with long dark hair like Hermione Granger's."

"Ooh, I know!" said Ellie's mum. "I've got a wig that would do the trick – I wore it to a Halloween party once. I'll go and see if I can find it."

"Thank you!" Katie replied.

Meanwhile, Jamila and Grace were putting together their outfits. Grace slipped into a leotard, a pink tutu, some white tights and ballet shoes, and tied her hair back into a rough bun.

"Wow, you look great!" said Jamila, who had started to read *Ballet Shoes* for her Booklover badge too.

Grace smiled, then curtseyed. "I love your party dress," she replied. Jamila had changed

71

into a pale blue dress with a pretty white collar.

"Thanks!" she said. "Mum made it for me.
I'm going to wear it with this," she said,
slipping a white pinny over the dress, which

Grace then tied at the
back.

Just then, Ellie's mum
reappeared with the
brown wig for Katie.
"Here you go, Katie! Now
Jamila, let's make a blue
headband for you. Then all
you'll need is some long

white socks and your school shoes."

It didn't take long for Ellie's mum to make
Jamila's headband out of some blue ribbon.
While she did that, Ellie and Grace helped
Charlie to make a pretend watch out of gold
paper stuck to a round piece of cardboard, as

well as a top hat, made out of black card.

"You're all going to look terrific!" said
Ellie's mum, as the girls gathered together
in their almost-final outfits.

"Thanks," they grinned.

"You'll need to take a group photo on the
day – I'm dying to see you all in your
finished outfits!" said Ellie's mum.

"We will!" The girls laughed.

On Sunday afternoon, Charlie and Boo sorted
through their books, deciding which ones to
donate to the Book Bonanza. But Charlie got
so engrossed in re-reading *Charlotte's Web* that
it was quite late by the time she sat down to
finish her Magic Shoes story.

Charlie read over what she'd already
written. How, she wondered, was Nibbles

going to discover that the trainers were magic and could help him escape from the car boot and get home again? Charlie looked out the window for inspiration. She watched a pair of birds playing on a tree branch. Then she daydreamed for a while, and wrote a couple more sentences about it being dark and Nibbles being hungry, then she looked at her watch.

Oh no! Half an hour had gone by and she was nowhere near being finished.

"Charlie!" Her mum came into her room. "It's time for supper, bath and bed soon," she said. "Put your homework away and come downstairs."

"But I can't," Charlie wailed. "I haven't finished my story!" She looked at her mum, tears welling up in her eyes. Then she told her all about how she'd been so busy reading her books that she hadn't got round to writing her story for school.

"Don't be upset, love," her mum soothed. "Did you say it had to be in on Wednesday?"

Charlie nodded. "At the latest."

"Well then," her mum said. "You can work on it tomorrow and, if you need to, you could always miss Brownies on Tuesday to finish it off."

"No!" Charlie sobbed. "I can't miss Brownies! If I do, I won't meet Holly Webb!"

Chapter 8

Charlie told the others all about her problem on Monday morning. "I tried to finish it yesterday," she sighed. "But I'm stuck on the ending!"

"Hmm... How about the trainers start talking to Nibbles," Jamila suggested.

"And they could start to jump up and down inside the boot of the car so that someone hears them!" suggested Grace.

"Good idea," said Ellie. "Then the boot is opened and Nibbles is brought back home to Charlie!"

"Perfect," said Katie.

"Thanks so much, you lot," said a grateful

76

Charlie. "I can't wait to get home and finish my story now. I wouldn't want to miss Holly Webb for anything!"

Charlie walked into the playground with a big grin on her face the next morning. Not only had she managed to finish her story, she'd even drawn a little picture of Nibbles with his nose poking out of a trainer to go with it.

"I couldn't have done it without you," Charlie confessed.

"That's what friends are for." Grace smiled, and gave her a hug.

"And now you can still come to Brownies!" said Katie.

"It wouldn't have been the same without you tonight," added Ellie.

"Yes," Jamila agreed. "You're Holly Webb's greatest fan!"

Charlie was so excited about Holly's visit that she and Boo were the first Brownies to arrive at the hall that night.

"Is Holly here yet?" Charlie asked as soon as she walked in.

"Not yet." Vicky smiled. "But keep a look out at the door. If you see her, you can be our official welcomer."

"OK!" Charlie grinned and took up her place at the entrance.

The Brownies arrived in dribs and drabs,

each one of them asking Charlie if Holly was there yet. Each time, Charlie shook her head. When the last Brownie arrived, the Leaders called all of them, except Charlie, into the Ring.

"We've got exciting news – we've managed to book the school hall for our Book Bonanza!" announced Vicky.

"Yaaaaay!" cheered the Brownies.

"So, we've printed some posters advertizing the event for you to colour in at home," Sam said, holding one up. "Can you put them up around town when they're finished?"

BROWNIE BOOK BONANZA

The Brownies nodded.

"Please tell as many people as possible about it – and gather lots of books to swap too," said Vicky.

79

Brownies

Next, Sam and Vicky invited the Brownies to tell their news, and Charlie listened in from her position at the door. Suddenly, a car pulled up outside and Charlie watched as a smiley lady she didn't recognize climbed out and walked towards the school hall. Could it be Holly…?

"Hello," the lady said. "I'm looking for the First Badenbridge Brownies."

"Are you Holly Webb?" Charlie gasped.

"I am," the lady replied. "Hello, I'm Charlie! Come in – I'll introduce you to Vicky and Sam."

Proudly, Charlie showed her into the hall. "Holly's here!" she said.

"Hi, Holly," said Vicky and Sam, shaking her hand.

"Come on, girls," said Vicky to the Brownies. "Let's give Holly a special Brownie welcome!"

Taking their Leaders' prompt, the Brownies stood up. They clapped and called "Welcome! Welcome! Welcome!" enthusiastically.

"Thank you, Brownies!" said Holly. "It's lovely to be here tonight – thanks for inviting me."

Holly settled into a seat between Vicky and Sam as they explained that the Sixes had come up with lots of questions to ask her, and invited the Hedgehogs to go first.

Lauren, their Sixer, introduced herself and then asked Holly when she did her writing.

"Whenever I can – mostly when my children are at school, and in the evenings, after they've gone to bed," Holly replied.

The Brownies were amazed to discover how Holly fitted her writing in around everything else she did.

Next, Molly asked the Rabbits' questions. They wanted to know how many books Holly had written.

"Er," said Holly, "I've written forty-three, I think…"

The Brownies gasped in astonishment. Charlie was particularly surprised – she had only just managed to finish *one* story, and couldn't imagine writing forty-three!

The next Six to ask their question was the Badgers. Izzy spoke for them, and asked Holly if she had always wanted to be an author.

"Well, I originally wanted to be a librarian. Then I decided to be an archaeologist, digging up ancient things. Then I changed my mind again and became an editor in a publishing house, which I did for six years."

Megan then asked, on behalf of the Squirrels, how Holly got her story ideas.

"I generally just think them up," Holly replied. "But now people quite often tell me good stories about animals, which is helpful."

Then it was the Hedgehogs' turn and Lauren asked, "So where do you do your writing?"

"On the sofa!" Holly replied.

The Brownies giggled as they thought of sitting at their desks at school, and wished that they could sit on sofas instead!

Finally, it was Emma's chance to ask the Foxes' question about whether Holly wrote

84

her books out by hand.

"That's a good question," said Holly. "I plan my stories in a notebook sometimes, but I usually write on a laptop. That said, my first book was written in a notebook, on trains."

The Brownies then wanted to know which book she wrote first, and if she had a favourite book or character. They were keen to tell Holly which books they liked best too.

When all their questions had been answered, Holly said she'd brought some things with her to show them. First, she produced the notebook she had mentioned earlier. Then, she pulled a big pile of paper out of her bag and handed sheets around the Ring.

85

"This is what my manuscript looks like after my editor has read it," said Holly. "You can see her comments written all around the edge of the page."

"So you mean your story changes?" Charlie asked.

Holly nodded. "Yes, sometimes my editor makes a suggestion to make the story work better, so I write a new draft."

Charlie was amazed – so, writing stories was often hard work for published authors too!

Next, Holly showed the Brownies some printed copies of her books, only the words on the cover and inside weren't in English!

"These are translations of my stories, which are published in other countries," Holly explained.

"They're amazing," said Lauren.

"I'm really sorry to interrupt," said Vicky.

"But we haven't got long before the end of our meeting…"

"Noooo!" the Brownies groaned.

Vicky, Sam and Daisy laughed along with Holly.

"Lots of you have brought copies of Holly's books with you that you would like her to sign – if you don't mind, Holly?" Vicky glanced across at her.

"I'd love to!" she replied.

And so the Brownies gathered round Holly and chatted to her as she signed their books.

"I think your animal stories are just
brilliant," said Charlie when it was her turn.
"I've read all of them!"

Holly smiled at her. "That's wonderful –
I'm flattered that you enjoy them so much."

When Holly had signed her book, Charlie
noticed Vicky and Sam beckoning her over.

"Charlie," said Vicky. "As you're Holly's
biggest fan, we thought you might like to
present these flowers to her to say thank you
for coming."

"Yes, please!" Charlie beamed.

When the last book had been signed, the
Brownies got back into their Ring.

"Now," said Vicky. "Don't forget to take a
Book Bonanza poster with you when you
leave. Daisy will hand them out at the door."

"Before we hold hands to sing 'Brownie
Bells'," added Sam, "Charlie has something

to say on our behalf."

Charlie stood up proudly and walked over to Holly with the flowers.

"On behalf of the First Badenbridge Brownies," Charlie said, "I'd like to thank you for coming to see us tonight. Oh – and for answering all our questions!"

"Thank you, Brownies," said Holly. "And have a great Book Bonanza!"

All the Brownies smiled and gave Holly a gigantic round of applause.

Chapter 9

"I can't believe I actually met Holly Webb," Charlie sighed, as they gathered in the playground on Wednesday morning.

"Wasn't she nice?" said Grace.

"I'm going to keep the book she signed for me for absolutely ever!" added Jamila.

"Me too," said Katie, as she watched Ellie rummaging around in her school bag. Finally, she pulled out a colourful sheet of paper. "Hey – what's that?"

"It's the Book Bonanza poster," Ellie explained. "I finished colouring it in this morning before school. I was going to ask if they'd put it up on the main door."

"Great idea," said Charlie.

"Let's ask Mr Cole – we can hand in our stories at the same time," said Grace.

They found Mr Cole in their classroom and told him all about meeting Holly Webb. Charlie showed him her signed book.

"She wished us luck with our Book Bonanza as well," added Grace. "It's going to be held in the hall the Saturday after next. May we put up Ellie's poster for it?"

"Of course!" Mr Cole said. "I'll bring in some books for you to swap too. It sounds like a really good cause."

"Thanks," the five girls replied.

In fact, over the next few days, lots of teachers mentioned the Book Bonanza, and put books in the donation box that Vicky had left in the staffroom on Tuesday night. Some of them said that they would also try to come along on Saturday.

Meanwhile, Jamila, Ellie, Grace, Katie and Charlie spent every spare moment busily reading their last two books, ready to be tested by Catherine at the library that coming weekend. And when they got together for tea at Grace and Katie's house on Friday afternoon, they took it in turns to pretend to be Catherine so that they could test each other.

When they met up with the real Catherine on Saturday morning, they told her all about meeting Holly and their news about the Book Bonanza.

"Do you think you'd be able to put up

one of our posters for it, please?" asked Grace, pulling one out of her bag, along with the *Nanny McPhee* DVD.

"Of course!" said Catherine, taking the poster and DVD. "I'll put it up in the entrance for everyone to see. Now, I seem to remember we were going to have a chat about some of those books you've been reading. Who's ready to be tested?"

"Me!" the five girls said.

"Come on then," Catherine replied. "Let's go and sit in that corner and you can tell me all about them."

The friends enjoyed talking to Catherine about the reference books they'd borrowed from the library the last time they visited. Catherine was interested to know if they'd

learned more about their hobbies through
their reading. Then they each chatted to her
about a fiction book they'd read. She
wondered how the books had made them feel;
if they'd made the girls laugh, or feel sad, or
even scared! At the end of their test, Catherine
presented the friends with two stickers each.
"I've read a great book today!" one of them said,
and *"I love books"* said the other.

Then Catherine wrote a quick
note for the girls to give to
Vicky and Sam at Brownies
to confirm that they had
been tested for part of their
badge work.

"Thanks for all your help," said Katie, as the
girls put their coats on, ready to head home.

"You're very welcome," Catherine told
them. "Come back and tell me how you got

on with the rest of your badge. And good luck with your Book Bonanza next week!"

It rained all day on Sunday, but Jamila, Katie, Grace, Ellie and Charlie didn't mind one bit. They spent the whole day tucked up in their cosy bedrooms, busily reading their last two books, which their Leaders were going to test them on.

At Brownies the following Tuesday, the girls gave Vicky and Sam the notes and stickers that Catherine had given them to show they had been successfully tested.

"Excellent," said Sam, making a note on her clipboard. "Just a bit more testing and you will have completed the reading section of your badge work. Do you think you can finish your books for next week, girls?"

"Definitely," Katie said confidently.

Vicky smiled. "Great! Now, why don't you go and help Daisy until the meeting starts?"

Daisy was over at the other end of the hall. She was sitting at a big table covered in piles of books and surrounded by boxes.

"Are these books for the Book Bonanza?" asked Jamila.

Daisy nodded. "We need to sort them into different categories."

"You mean like children's books, reference books or recipe books?" said Danuta, coming over to join them.

"Exactly," replied Daisy. "I've already put labels on the front of the boxes, so it shouldn't take long to put the books in the right ones."

The Brownies got to work. With everyone helping out, the job was soon done, and Vicky and Sam thanked them all for their help when they gathered for their Pow Wow a bit later.

"Did you all enjoy meeting Holly last week?" Vicky asked.

The Brownies nodded.

"She said she had a fab time too," said Sam.

"But tonight we've got some Booklover badge work to do," Vicky continued. "And, if we've got time later, Daisy has said she'll help us make a Book Bonanza banner to go over the door on Saturday."

"First, though, let's tackle the book care section of your badge," said Sam.

"This section of the badge requires you to know how to look after your books and keep them clean and smart," explained Vicky. "A way to do that is to make a cover for your books, like these two."

Vicky held them up. One book had been covered with colourful wrapping paper. The other had been covered with plain paper that had been decorated by hand with felt-tip pens, glitter and gem stickers.

"We've brought each of you a little notebook," Sam went on, "and we'd like you to cover and decorate it however you like. You can use the notebooks to record all the books you read in future."

The Brownies grinned excitedly.

"We've put lots of paper, stickers, felt-tip pens and glue on your Six tables," said Vicky. "As you work, Sam and I will come round to see how you are doing, and chat to you about how you look after the books at school and your own ones at home."

The hall was soon alive with busy Brownies, working away on their book covers. As they coloured, cut and stuck, Vicky and Sam spoke to each of the Sixes about how to store books safely on shelves and how to protect books

Brownies

from damage as you use them. The Leaders
seemed pleased that the Brownies were so
careful with their books and congratulated all
of them on completing that section of the
badge. After each girl had finished her book
cover and showed it to Vicky and Sam, they
went over to help Daisy, who was working on
the large Book Bonanza banner.

Soon, they had the most colourful banner they'd ever seen – no one in Badenbridge would be able to miss it!

"That looks great, girls!" said Vicky, admiring their work. "And you've finished it just in time to go home."

The Brownies sighed. They didn't want to go home yet!

Sam smiled. "Come on, get your things together. And take a copy of this letter before you go; it contains all the information you need about the Book Bonanza on Saturday."

On World Book Day the following Thursday, Badenbridge Primary was greeted by a colourful collection of book characters. All the pupils (and the teachers too) looked spectacular in their costumes. Mr Cole was

Dennis the Menace and Mrs Sadler, Badenbridge Primary's head teacher, was dressed as Professor McGonagall, complete with a splendid pointy black hat. Katie was a bit annoyed when she discovered that two other girls were also dressed as Hermione, but she soon saw the funny side of it! And poor Grace had to accept that six girls in Reception had come as Angelina Ballerina

and looked almost identical to her as Posy Fossil! No one else had come as Pippi Longstocking, though and Ellie's plaits got lots of attention. Jamila teamed up with a White Rabbit (a girl in Year 4) during a group photo that Mrs Sadler took, and Charlie, as Doctor Doolittle, "spoke" in barks and growls to three girls from Year 1 who were all dressed as Spot the Dog.

And when school finally started, the book-action was non-stop: from book quizzes and story-telling to a maths quiz based on characters in fairy stories, there was something for everyone at Badenbridge Primary to enjoy.

At the end of the day, everyone gathered in the hall for a special assembly to announce the winner of the Magic Shoes writing competition.

"You all wrote terrific stories," said Mrs Sadler. "We were really impressed by the high standard of your writing. Some of you even managed to illustrate your stories, which was wonderful! So thank you for all your hard work, everyone. But there can only be one winner, I'm afraid…"

The room fell silent.

"…And that is … Boo!"

"Yessss!" The Brownies cheered and clapped the loudest of anyone in the hall as Boo, dressed as Dorothy from *The Wizard of Oz*, went up to collect her prize. Boo was thrilled, and Charlie could not have been prouder of her big sister.

Chapter 10

After all the excitement of the last two
weeks, the Brownies couldn't quite believe
that there was going to be even more on
Saturday – Book Bonanza day!

Jamila, Charlie, Katie, Grace and Ellie
turned up, together with Boo, at the hall at
nine o'clock, just as their Leaders had
asked. Along with the other girls, they
carried the boxes of books from the
staffroom, where they had been allowed to
store them until now, over to the hall. But
they hadn't been there long before people
started to arrive. Lots of them!

"Oh no," said Charlie. "They're early!

Book Bonanza hasn't started yet!"

Vicky and Sam went over to speak to the grown-ups, who looked very surprised to see all the Brownies.

"What's going on?" wondered Grace.

"I'll go and see if Daisy knows what's happening," said Jamila, running over to her.

Daisy looked worried. "There's been a mix-up," she said. "This is the Badenbridge Community Choir, and they booked the hall for a rehearsal this morning. They're meant to finish at the same time we open our Book Bonanza – only no one thought about us needing time to set up!"

Just then, the other four friends arrived at Jamila's side.

"But we've got so much to do," said Grace. "It's going to take us ages to arrange the hall properly!"

"And we've put loads of posters up telling people when we open!" pointed out Charlie.

"They'll just have to cancel their rehearsal," declared Katie. "Our Book Bonanza is more important!"

"But this is their last rehearsal before a competition they're in next week!" said Daisy.

After some discussion with the choir leader, Vicky and Sam called the Brownies over to one side of the hall.

"OK," said Sam. "You've all heard that there's been a mix-up with the hall this morning. But we've come up with a plan!"

Vicky explained that the choir had agreed to finish their rehearsal half an hour before the Book Bonanza was due to open. Then they would help the Brownies lay out their books, and had even offered to make and sell cups of tea and coffee to help raise more funds for Book Aid International. After the first hour of the Book Bonanza, the choir would get up on stage and sing. That way, they'd be able to do a run-through of their performance for the competition with an audience, and the Brownies would still be able to hold their book swap!

"If we all join in, we'll get everything done!" stated Vicky. "Remember, you're going to have to set up really quietly while the choir are rehearsing. Do your best, Brownies!"

The Brownies quietly set about putting labels out on the tables while the choir practised. Meanwhile, some of the girls went out to help their Leaders and Daisy hang the splendid banner over the hall door. Eventually, the choir finished their rehearsal and there was a frantic rush to get things ready. But the choir members were really helpful and the tables were soon covered in brilliant books.

"There're people queuing outside!" said Pip, racing into the hall.

"Are we ready?" asked Sam, looking around.

"Yes!" the Brownies and the choir declared.

"Then let the Book Bonanza begin!" Sam opened the doors of the hall to allow the flood of people in.

During the first hour, the Brownies took lots of money on the door, the choir took donations for their hot drinks, and the visitors swapped masses of books. Some people didn't bring books to swap, but donated money to Book Aid International to buy books instead.

Vicky and Sam took over the job of selling hot drinks when the choir took their places on

stage to perform to the packed hall. And when they completed their final song, the Brownies clapped louder than anyone else.

A short while later, after the last book-swapper had left and when the choir had helped them tidy up the hall, the Brownies chatted about their busy morning.

"So many people came," said Grace.

"And lots of teachers from school too!" added Jamila.

"Mr Cole picked up a recipe book from my table," said Katie.

"Did you all manage to get a book?" asked Daisy.

They nodded and showed her the books they'd found: Charlie had an encyclopaedia of cats, and

Grace had found a book about world dance. Jamila had

found two books: one on cookery for children and another about folk music, while Katie was delighted

to have picked up a book about athletics and Ellie was equally pleased because she'd found a book on French painters.

114

"Brownies!" Vicky and Sam called. They were standing in the middle of the hall with their rights hands up.

"Well done, girls — and choir too! You did a great job," Vicky said. "And good luck in your competition next week."

"Yes," agreed Sam. "We overcame our double-booking problem and we've cleared almost everything!"

"What are we going to do with the left-over books?" asked Ashvini.

"The man who runs the second-hand bookshop in town has said he'll give Book Aid International a generous donation in exchange for them," explained Vicky.

The Brownies clapped.

"So," said Sam, "let's put away these last few tables, and then you'd better get ready for your parents to pick you up."

The next couple of days passed slowly after all the excitement of the week before – the Brownies couldn't wait to find out how much money they'd raised for Book Aid International! They sat expectantly in the Ring for their Pow Wow the following Tuesday. Vicky and Sam thanked them all again for their hard work, and then announced that they had collected just over £300.

"Hooray!" the Brownies cheered.

"That will buy a hundred and fifty books for children in Africa!" said Vicky.

"You did really well, girls. And you were very calm after the mix-up with the booking of the hall," Sam added. "Vicky and I are really proud of you."

"Yes," said Vicky. "It's a good job Brownies always remain calm in a crisis! Let's hope the Badenbridge Community Choir has as much success with their competition as we've had with our Book Bonanza – they said they would let us know the result, so we'll keep you posted."

"Now, we've got just a few more bits of testing to do for your Booklover badge," announced Sam.

The Brownies realized that they were very close to finishing their badge work – they couldn't wait!

"On your Six tables you'll find some book-title word searches to keep you busy while we make our way round to test everyone on your last two books," explained Vicky. "Off you go!"

The word search was quite hard and the Brownies had to help each other to complete it. Meanwhile, Vicky and Sam spoke to the individual Brownies about the last two books they had read. Then Vicky and Sam checked with each Brownie, one by one, to see if they had completed all the tasks of their Booklover badge.

"Well, what brilliant girls we have here at First Badenbridge Brownies," said Vicky, once the Brownies had gathered back in the Brownie Ring.

Sam agreed. "Every single one of you has done an incredible amount of reading and book work – and I'm very pleased to award you all your Booklover badge! Well done!"

"Yay!" the Brownies cheered, giving themselves a big clap!

As the five best friends stood at the hall door at the end of their Brownie meeting, waiting for their parents to collect them, they

admired their Booklover badges. They were impatient to get them sewn on to their Brownie clothes.

"I've really enjoyed working on this badge," Grace said.

"And Book Bonanza too," added Jamila.

"Meeting Holly Webb was my favourite bit of our World Book Day celebrations," said Charlie.

"I liked discovering new authors," Ellie declared.

"Hey, you know two of the best things in the world begin with 'b'," Katie pointed out.

Her best friends looked at her and grinned.

"Brownies and books!" they all cheered at once.

Join the Brownies

Brownies do it all!

They do cool things to get badges like the Artist badge and the Computer badge, they have sleepovers, they make heaps of friends and have lots of fun.

Brownies are aged from seven to ten and are part of Girlguiding UK, the largest organisation for girls and young women in the UK, which has around half a million members and supporters.

To learn more about what Brownies get up to, visit www.girlguiding.org.uk/brownies or call 0800 169 5901 to find out how you can join in the fun.

How Charlie got her Booklover badge!

1. Chose four books she had recently enjoyed. Charlie talked about what she liked about the books with her testers.

2. Read two more books by different authors, and chatted with her testers about them.

3. Made a bookmark and learned how to make a book cover. She talked with Vicky about how to look after books.

4. Chose a reference book, and showed her tester that she knew how to use it.

5. Made a poster about the library, including details like opening times and what you could borrow.

Booklover

How to make a Book Journal!

You will need:

* A rectangle of colourful wrapping paper that is at least one-and-a-half times taller and wider than the book you want to cover
* Some sticky tape
* Coloured pens and pencils
* Decorative stickers, ribbons and glue

1. If your wrapping paper has a pattern on one side, place it decorative side down, then position your open book in the middle of the paper.

2. Holding the book firmly in position, fold the top of the paper down and gently mark the crease where it touches the book. Do the same with the bottom end of paper.

3. Put the book to one side and then, using the creases as guides, fold the paper in across both the top and the bottom, like this.

4. Now place your book back in the middle of the wrapping paper. Take one of the sides of your new wrapping paper cover and fold it over the original back cover of the book. You have now made a little sleeve.

5. Holding the back of the book inside the sleeve, open the book's front cover and fold the wrapping paper cover over that side too. It's important to do this with the book open, especially if your book has a wide spine, otherwise the cover will be too tight. Now tuck the front of the book into the second sleeve you have made.

6. Close the book and you will have made a brand new cover! If you want to, you can secure the wrapping paper cover in position with sticky tape inside the front and back of the book.

7. Decorate your new book cover by colouring or stickering it. If your book has a wide spine, you could glue a piece of ribbon along it.

You can now use your beautifully-covered journal to record the books that you read and make notes of what you liked about them!

Collect all the books in the series!

Brownies
Perfect Promise
Caroline Plaisted

Got it!
○

Brownies
Helping Hands
Caroline Plaisted

Got it!
○

Brownies
Sleepover Surprise
Caroline Plaisted

Got it!
○

Brownies
Friends Forever
Caroline Plaisted

Got it!

Brownies
Dance Dash
Caroline Plaisted

Got it!

Brownies
Circus Camp
Caroline Plaisted

Got it!

Brownies
Christmas Cheer
Caroline Plaisted

Got it!